This book
belongs to:

_____

MADAME
Badobedah

For Jamie, Lyra, and Margot: the adventurer crew.
With all my love
S. D.

For S. T. H. with love and art heists
L. O'H.

Text copyright © 2019 by Sophie Dahl
Illustrations copyright © 2019 by Lauren O'Hara

First U.S. edition 2020

Library of Congress Catalog Card Number pending
ISBN 978-1-5362-1022-4

20 21 22 23 24 25 APS 10 9 8 7 6 5 4 3 2 1

Printed in Humen, Dongguan, China

This book was typeset in Joanna.
The illustrations were done in watercolor.

Walker Books US
a division of
Candlewick Press
99 Dover Street
Somerville, Massachusetts 02144

www.walkerbooksus.com

SOPHIE DAHL

MADAME
Badobedah

illustrated by
LAUREN
O'HARA

WALKER BOOKS

Part One
The New (Old) Guest

My name is Mabel.

I live somewhere curious.

It's called the Mermaid Hotel.

My dad is the manager, but my mom is the *boss*.

Our back door leads to the sea, along a path of

old-men trees, battered and bent by the wind and salt.

Rock thyme twines with thistles that spike your feet if you're barefoot. But I don't care because I'm an adventurer.

And adventurers are often shoeless.

As well as
bare feet, adventurers
like:

Swiss cheese,

the number eight,

donkeys,

and popovers. Yum, popovers.

Adventurers *don't* like:

being told
what to do,

spiders,

ham,

and gym shoes (because they smell like cardboard boxes).
Mine are too tight. They sit at school in a box with all the
other smelly gym shoes for company.

I am an only child. I can cross my eyes. And sometimes,
when I write, I get my *d*'s and *b*'s mixed up. My teacher,
Mrs. Banks, says, "Mabel, your *d* is dancing to the beat of a *b*!"
And then she laughs. Bad joke.

I prefer home. No shoes; more bare feet. And adventure.
Lots of lovely adventure.

THE
Mermaid Hotel

Although the Mermaid Hotel is called a hotel, it's really a bed-and-breakfast.

This means you get a *bed* and *breakfast* but you have to make your own lunch and dinner.

The hotel has bothersome seagulls that shriek on the sills. And a mermaid over the front door that I call Beryl in Peril because she's far from the sea, waving.

And inside: little packets of marmalade and butter that I hide in my pocket because they make a good snack.

But most importantly, the Mermaid Hotel has *guests*: strangers who come and go. Some are delightful; some are like ham.

I am not a guest. I am a *resident*.

I'm going to tell you the story of our most interesting guest.

I was sitting under the front desk, minding my own business, when the bell rang. RIIIIIIIIIIIIIIIIIIING!

I peered up.

She was old, old, old. With red lips.

She was not alone. She had

two dogs,

two cats,

a tortoise,

and twenty-three bags, all clustered around her like a choir.

I thought she might be a little bit awful.

"*Darlink,*" she growled, "please remove yourself from under the desk and pass me my bag. The blue one there, to the right of that terrifically ugly coat stand. No, you frightful little child, not that one! Blue, I said!"

I passed her the bag. It felt like it had ten gold bars in it. I might have given her an icy glare. No one had ever called me such names before, and I A-DORE that coat stand.

The awful stranger didn't say thank you.

Behind her trailed the
smells of old roses, spice, and
vanilla. Her hair was red and crunchy,
like a candy apple without the stickiness. She
wore a cloud of feathers around her neck. Her head poked
out like an angry ostrich pecking for grubs.

That was when I named her Madame Badobedah (rhymes with *ooooh la la*). A good name for the growly-voiced, suitcase-heavy, feather-clad guest who I was one hundred and ten percent sure was a *villain*.

Two big trunks, one dressing table, the twenty-three bags (even the dogs had bags!), thirteen boxes, and *hundreds* of trinkets, all spilling down the hall after her.

"Good grief, all this . . . this *stuff*!" my mom muttered as she and Dad staggered up the stairs. Madame Badobedah walked silently behind, arrow-straight, carrying nothing but a cushion with her tortoise balanced on it like a precious, scaly emerald. She slipped a toffee into her mouth; she didn't offer me one.

We stopped outside Room 32.

Room 32 has a bedroom and a sitting room, one bath, one sink, one toaster, and seven teacups but only four saucers. Room 32 has an extraordinary secret, too, but I'm not going to tell you that right now.

I know this because I know *all* the rooms at the Mermaid Hotel, along with their secrets. I don't have brothers and sisters; I have rooms. A room can be a lot like a person: it sees stories and parties and lazy days and birthday cakes. And sometimes it sees sad things, too.

So, with its secrets and saucers, Room 32 now also had Madame Badobedah, two dogs, two cats, a tortoise, and Madame Badobedah's secrets. A whole heap of them.

12

Room 32

"It was like a circus!" my mom said later. "Rude woman."

"*Poor* woman," my dad said. I wondered what he meant.

"Those *trunks!*" Mom said.

I thought those trunks were full of stolen gold. That dressing table was spitting jewels. *She's not on vacation,* I thought. Oh, *this one is never leaving.*

I decided I'd better keep an eye out to see what that old sneak was up to.

"I'm just going upstairs to find a book!" I shouted.

"In a spy costume?" my dad asked.

"I'm wearing a raincoat and sunglasses because the weather forecast is varied," I said.

"Whatever you say, Mabel," Dad replied.

When a guest comes to stay, I'm not allowed to go into their room anymore because it suddenly belongs to them and is *private*.

But the hotel is, after all, where I live. A guest is just borrowing the room, really. So sometimes I peek through the keyhole a bit, to see what's happening. Then I am not just Mabel, but Mabel the Spy.

And spies *spy.*

To be the best spy, you need to be really good at
observing people: what they are like, what habits they
have. A habit is something that is hard to give up. I have
the habit of biting my nails. Nails are so chewy and hard
and delicious. I *might* also have the habit of picking my
nose and wiping it on the wall.

And, after observing

Madame Badobedah through the keyhole for a whole

three and a half minutes, I had a strong theory about her:

SHE WAS, WITHOUT QUESTION, AN ANCIENT

SUPERVILLAIN ON THE RUN FROM THE POLICE.

(Her chosen hideout: Room 32, the Mermaid Hotel.)

This was the evidence:

1. The fugitive looked around the room. She pulled out a pair of ballet shoes from one of the many trunks. She kissed them. Clearly she did ballet to get all limber for breaking and entering and for catapulting through museums in a catsuit.

2. A shopping list of strangeness exploded from her bags—a glimmering tiara, one ice skate, a Hawaiian lei, and a pack of cards. Curious.

3. The fugitive hid a pile of coins under her bed, in a sock. She arranged the lei over it. She'd obviously brought it to remind her of her family, who were waiting for her in Honolulu. She'd join them when the coast was clear.

4. A police car whistled past in the distance. She sank down as though she was hiding. And then the strangest thing happened: Madame Badobedah sat on the bed and cried.

I studied her for days. This is what I learned:

1. Madame Badobedah never went outside. Not ever.

2. No one knew her name. All the grown-ups called her
Mrs. *mutter, mutter*. They seemed invisible to her. We all were.

3. That tortoise was the most suspicious creature I'd ever seen.
He had beady little eyes and he scurried around the corridors
like a dizzy chicken. He ate bananas from her fingers, and
bananas are *revolting*.

4. She did not say "darling" like anyone I knew. *Darlink.* It was pure menace, whispered like an insult.

5. She wore two pairs of socks on each foot. Underneath the socks, her toes were long and purple-ish with knobs on them. They were grim. They were, in fact, the toes of a villain.

Since no one else seemed to care that
we were living with a high priestess
of crime, I realized I was on my own,
as usual. I would have to wait for the
chance to catch her red-handed.

Part Two
Sailing the High Seas

One Saturday morning

I got in position again, stationed outside Room 32,
and sat patiently scratching a hole in the carpet
with my foot.

Spies are patient, you see.

This time — oh my! — Madame Badobedah

opened the door. She seemed to know I was on the other side.

I pretended I was looking for a lost button.

24

"My favorite button," I said sadly, to the air. "Oh, where are you, dear button?"

Madame Badobedah said, "Would you like a cup of tea, *darlink?*"

"All right," I said. Even though I was a teeny bit scared. "But I'm not officially allowed to have tea. It wakes you up like billy-o, you know."

"Billy-o? What fun! Perhaps an unofficial sip? Your name is Mabel, isn't it?"

My heart was thudding. She knew my name! I followed her into Room 32. It felt different. It was bigger, cartoon-colored; alive somehow.

The fire was roaring even though the sun outside was shining, and that shifty tortoise skittered along the floor like a man on a mission. Scratchy music played on a magic box.

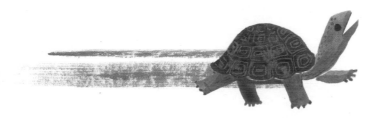

Madame Badobedah's dressing table stood up against the wall as if it had always been there. Pots and cloudy puffs and lipsticks sat on top, in the shadow of a huge bottle of perfume that read *Shalimar*. There were something like 507 drawers.

I wanted to know *what* was in those drawers. It itched inside of me. I asked her, like I didn't care, "So, what's in your drawers?"

"Diamonds, coins from Cleopatra's tomb, things like that," Madame Badobedah said. My heart did a swan dive. I wore my best spy face, where my eyes give nothing away.

"Hmm," I said.

She poured me a cup of tea from a teapot that was wearing a sweater. "Even he feels the cold in this blasted country, the poor *darlink*," she said.

The bed in Room 32 looked like a pirate ship. I decided it was time to put Madame Badobedah's villainy to the test.

"Do you know who Anne Bonny was?" I asked her.

"Questions, questions! No, why don't you tell me?" said Madame Badobedah.

"Anne was one of the most fearsome pirates of all time. She liked stealing gold. Probably kept it in socks." I stared into her eyes. I bet she had a picture of Anne Bonny in a heart-shaped frame somewhere.

"I'm a big fan of gold," Madame Badobedah replied smoothly. "She sounds marvelous. That bed of mine is a pirate ship—I call it the *Not-So-Jolly Roger*. Shall we set sail, Captain Mabel?"

I thought about it.

"Aye aye!" I said.

I heard the seagulls cry, and somewhere in the distance a sea shanty echoed through the mist.

The *Not-So-Jolly Roger* crew was weary after months at sea; the ship was creaking with jewels, coins, and exotic animals. There was a dodo in the dinghy, and a one-eyed parrot snored soundly on the cannon.

It was the first mate who spied the approaching storm as she fed her cats anchovies. (Yuck, anchovies: spiny and disgusting.)

"There's a storm a-rollin' in, Captain Darlink!" the first mate hollered. "What is your command?"

"Stay calm, fellow!" I shouted. "Secure the animals safely in the hold! And for pity's sake, put the rubies in your bloomers!"

I steered the ship through
writing waves and slashing rain, past a
rainbow-colored serpent and a school of
flying fish.

"I need a toffee, too. Sweets are vital in
a storm!" I bellowed as I saw that sneaky
first mate pop one into her mouth.

I navigated my trusty ship around
the treacherous rocks, leaning in as we
missed them by a breath. And as the
sun rose, we saw the green of land,
and the animals sighed with relief.
I straightened my hat as we docked.
The tortoise (whose name is Boris)
was a bit green around the gills
and wobbly on his feet.

It had been a successful voyage.

Then I remembered that, while she might
be a good first mate, Madame Badobedah
was still a villain—most probably a *very*
dangerous criminal. Also, the room smelled
of anchovies. Time to escape. "Take care of
your bloomers!" I said, and ran downstairs.

Part Two (and a half)

Prehistoric Bones and the Excuses Grown-ups Make

All the grown-ups said that

Madame Badobedah was rude. My dad said she

was rude because she was lonely. My mom said she

thought she was a princess. I remembered her tiara.

Sometimes, before school, I was allowed to take the villain her toast and marmalade in bed.

"Come in, Captain Mabel!" Madame Badobedah would say, her voice a mixture of honey and sea stones all clanking together in a jar. She'd sit up in bed with a cough and a rattle. "A quick game of Old Maid before school? And *darlink*, could you open the curtains, please? I'm prehistoric and I don't think my bones have woken up yet."

If it was raining, which it did a lot, she'd say, "Oh, well. I shall just stay in the pirate ship *all day*." And she'd pull the covers up to her chin.

I think this was her big excuse to lurk inside all day, guarding her money sock. The weather is often used as an excuse by grown-ups.

Once, the phone rang and she picked it up and snapped, "No, I simply can't meet you at midday. I'm ludicrously busy." I held my breath. She snuggled back down into bed and winked at me.

Busyness is another well-known grown-up excuse. But lying and avoiding people? Hmm. *Shady lady.*

Part Three
The Place Where Mermaids Swim

When she was a girl,

before she was an international jewel thief . . .

Madame Badobedah crossed the
sea on a big ship, because there
was a war.

She told me this as we drank hot chocolate and ate cookies on her bed. "When my ship docked in New York, I could still feel the ground moving under my feet for two whole weeks, even though I was on dry land. It was most strange!"

Madame Badobedah was a ballerina when she was young. She showed me how she could walk with a book balanced on her head. The book perched on her nest of hair like a sparrow. "I was the Sugar Plum Fairy in *The Nutcracker!*" she said. "I wore a jeweled tiara. And once, I was so poor that I had to eat bread soup because the only thing in the cupboard was dry bread!" She laughed, spraying cookie crumbs onto the cats and dogs.

She said a man she once knew always
called her "my sweetheart." I think it was her
husband, who is probably wearing shorts and waiting
for her in the tropical breeze with the rest of her family.

She said a mountain of people asked for her hand. "But
get that ring on your finger and he'll want the whole *arm*,
darlink! It's verrrrrrrry important for a woman to be
independent, Captain Mabel. This you should know!"

I told her I could hold my breath underwater in
the bath for forty-three seconds. This might
be a lie.

"Because you're brilliant," Madame
Badobedah said. "Can you ice-skate?"

"No," I said.

"I used to love it. I'd skate on a river in the winter with my cousin Olga, and we would swim in that very same river in the summer." Madame Badobedah poured me another cup. "Olga's eyes were the color of shiny black beetles and she *hated* saying sorry." She laughed. "It's so important in life to say sorry if one has gone wrong, *darlink*."

"Grown-ups never say sorry, really," I answered. "But they expect children to do it all the time." I stroked Boris's scaly little foot.

"Well, Mabel, I want to say sorry to *you*," Madame Badobedah said. "I'm truly sorry I was grumpy and foul and said dreadful things to you when I first arrived. I was afraid of this new place and starting again. I'm so old to start again."

"It's OK," I said. I realized then that I really quite liked her. Even though she was on the run, with her funny habits and her strange toes and her banana-eating tortoise. Sneaky old villain. I took a deep breath. "You don't even know the best secret about the Mermaid Hotel yet," I said. "It's in this room. It's even better than the pirate ship."

Madame Badobedah's eyes lit up.

"I'll take you. No one knows how to get there but me," I whispered, taking her soft, gnarled hand.

"I'm honored," the villain said. "I'm ready. A boiled sweet for the road, Captain?" She gave me a lemon barley candy from the tin, all sneezy with powdered sugar. I pushed against a panel on the wall, and a door opened.

"You thought it was just an extra closet!" I said as we crawled in past the quiet and shushing dresses, and she laughed and said, "I did! Oof, my knees!"

"Are you all right, or do you need oiling?" I asked her.

"Oh, creaking is like laughing, my sweet. It means you're having fun," Madame Badobedah said. We slithered through a jungle of bags and shoes and I was pricked by a safety pin and we had to administer first aid with a tin box, some tissues, and an old toffee.

"Being an adventurer can be dangerous," Madame Badobedah said. "But exactly the right kind of danger, *darlink*."

We had reached the end of the closet, where the last rafter met the ceiling. I knocked on it three times, and the mermaids answered me. They always do. They sang through the walls and their voices were sweet.

"The mermaids say you're a friend," I told Madame Badobedah, and she grinned, her teeth shining in the dark.

"I am," she said. I'd never seen her grin before.

"Shut your eyes and count to ten, please."

Madame Badobedah counted slowly.

"Now open."

Her eyes grew big.
"Oh, Mabel, how wonderful!"
she said.

"Feel that balmy breeze! Look, there's the pirate ship in the cove! And what's this? Oh, a waterfall! It's heaven. I'm so thrilled I brought my bathing costume!"

Madame Badobedah floated in the pool, drinking from a coconut, and the mermaids combed and braided my hair and told me they'd missed me.

"My cousin Olga would have adored it here," Madame Badobedah said, kicking her legs. "Simply adored it."

We were building a sandcastle and plotting a dive for pearls when I heard my mom call "MA-BEL!" up the stairs in her I-mean-business voice, so we had to tear ourselves away from paradise, crawling double-quick back through the dresses.

I shouted, "I'm coming, Mom!" and that was when Madame Badobedah picked up something from her dresser and handed it to me. It was a huge, shimmering, real-life pearl. She closed my fingers around it and said, "A present. For you, adventurer."

I gasped. I wondered if it was from one of her heists. I don't know anyone else with precious jewels just hanging about. "Thank you," I said.

I didn't want to leave her. I wondered what she'd do when I was gone. She would sit by the window, I thought, with the dogs at her feet, and look out at the sea. She would say it was "*achy-bones cold*" and wrap a quilt around herself. Madame Badobedah says I have good bones and an old soul. She talks about bones a lot: old ones, good ones, cold ones, aching ones.

After my bath, I snuck up for a game of Old Maid on the pirate ship. We were both in our nighties. I wore my sunglasses so my eyes wouldn't give me away, and when I won, Madame Badobedah cried, "VILLAINESS!" and then she smiled a great big smile, as big as the sky.

"But *you* are the villain!" I said. "Robber royalty." I took the sunglasses off. They had polka dots. Madame Badobedah has big green eyes with purple crinkles underneath.

"Gosh, am I?" she said. "A villain? My children certainly think I am." I didn't know she had children. They'd never come to visit.

"You steal jewels and rob pyramids and are on the run with your animals," I said in a rush. "The Mermaid Hotel is your hideout. You'll be reunited with your husband one day on an island in the sun. I've figured it all out."

"Reunited?" There was a long pause.

She looked toward the sea, as she always did. Then she looked me dead in the eyes.

"Well, Captain, you've found me out, *darlink*," she said. "There's nowhere for me to run. Can we keep it between us? I'd like to live out my last days peacefully."

I thought about Madame Badobedah's lovely smile, how she swims with mermaids, owns a tortoise named Boris, is never without a toffee, and always lets me be the captain. I thought about how she says sorry like she means it, has a perfume with a brave horse's name, *Shalimar*, and how she could pirouette through Cleopatra's tomb, arms full of treasure. I thought about pearls and bones and rainy days. I couldn't imagine anyone else would bring her toast and marmalade in prison. I'd be her only visitor.

"OK," I said finally, smiling at her. "It's a deal."

I'm going to sleep with Madame Badobedah's pearl for the rest of my life. I hid it under my pillow, stroking its cool roundness. I wondered if I would dream of mermaids.

What does Madame Badobedah dream of? Does she ice-skate with Olga, or sail the rocky seas toward the island where her family waits? And in those dreams, is she old or is she a child?

What I do know is this: Madame Badobedah
sleeps under the same roof as me. We dream at
the same time. Her real name is Irena. She told
me as I said good night.